About the Author

Tracey has been writing since childhood and won a public-speaking competition with one of her short stories when she was eleven years old. Her stories for children combine a love of writing with her passion for animals and simple concepts which children and young readers can engage with and understand.

She has a Graduate Diploma in Integrative Counselling and is the Medicines Management Site Coordinator at St Luke's Hospice in Sheffield, where she lives with her family and their eclectic mix of animals (including Sansa the Skunk).

Tracey Barker

SANSA

(the Not-So-Smelly Skunk)

AUSTIN MACAULEY PUBLISHERS™
LONDON * CAMBRIDGE * NEW YORK * SHARJAH

A CIP catalogue record for this title is available from the British Library.

ISBN 9781787103221 (Paperback)
ISBN 9781787103238 (E-Book)
www.austinmacauley.com

First Published (2018)
Austin Macauley Publishers™ Ltd.
25 Canada Square
Canary Wharf
London
E14 5LQ

Dedication

For Dad and all of my 'forever friends'.

Sansa the skunk sleeps in the hay
I wonder if she'd like to play
Shhh... quiet now, she's very shy
Whisper her name, give it a try...

I think it worked, I hear a sound
Her nose pops out to sniff the ground
Next, her head as she sniffs the air
See her lovely snow white hair.

The stripe is faint across her back
(Most other skunks are white and black)
She has a stretch and then a yawn
And heads off to a field of corn.

Sansa's tail is long and wide
It's hard to find a place to hide
She sees a bug, we hear a crunch
'Yum, that was breakfast, what's for lunch?'

See her stomp and run away?
She's telling us she wants to play
She needs to find someone who'll say
Sansa, be my friend today.

He has long ears, fur soft and grey
His burrow is close as he hops away
Hop, Hop, Hop. Who could it be?
"Hello rabbit, would you like to play?"
"No not with your smelly spray.
Go away!"

Hop
Hop
Hop

He's small and white, she takes a peek
He runs away and makes a squeak
Squeak, Squeak, Squeak. Who could it be?
"Hello mouse, would you like to play?"
"No not with your smelly spray.
Go away!"

She licks her paw to clean her face
Sees the mouse and starts to chase
Meeooow. Who could it be?
"Hello cat, would you like to play?"
"No not with your smelly spray.
Go away!"

squeak
squeak
squeak ...

Twit twoo ...

Here's a bird who's very wise
Who blinks and stares with yellow eyes
Twit Twoo. Who could it be?
"Hello owl, would you like to play?"
"No not with your smelly spray.
Go away!"

She finds him playing in the park
He sees the skunk and starts to bark
Woof, Woof, Woof. Who could it be?
"Hello dog, would you like to play?"
"No not with your smelly spray.
Go away!"

Woof
Woof
Woof

Sansa is hurt by what they say
They take one look and run away
She'd tell them if they really cared
She only sprays when she's very scared.

Sansa sits, she's all alone
She gives a sigh and heads for home
Through the wood where no one sees
'Wait, who's that hiding in the trees?'
Sigh...

A pointed nose, he's **black** and white
He has a stripe and looks just right
He does a stomp and runs away
Sansa knows it's time to play.

It's night time now, the moon is out
The skunks look up with pointed snouts
They play and play all through the night
But must be home before it's light.

They hurry home, it's almost dawn
Can you see them in the corn?
They're tired now from all the play
And snuggle up in the cosy hay.

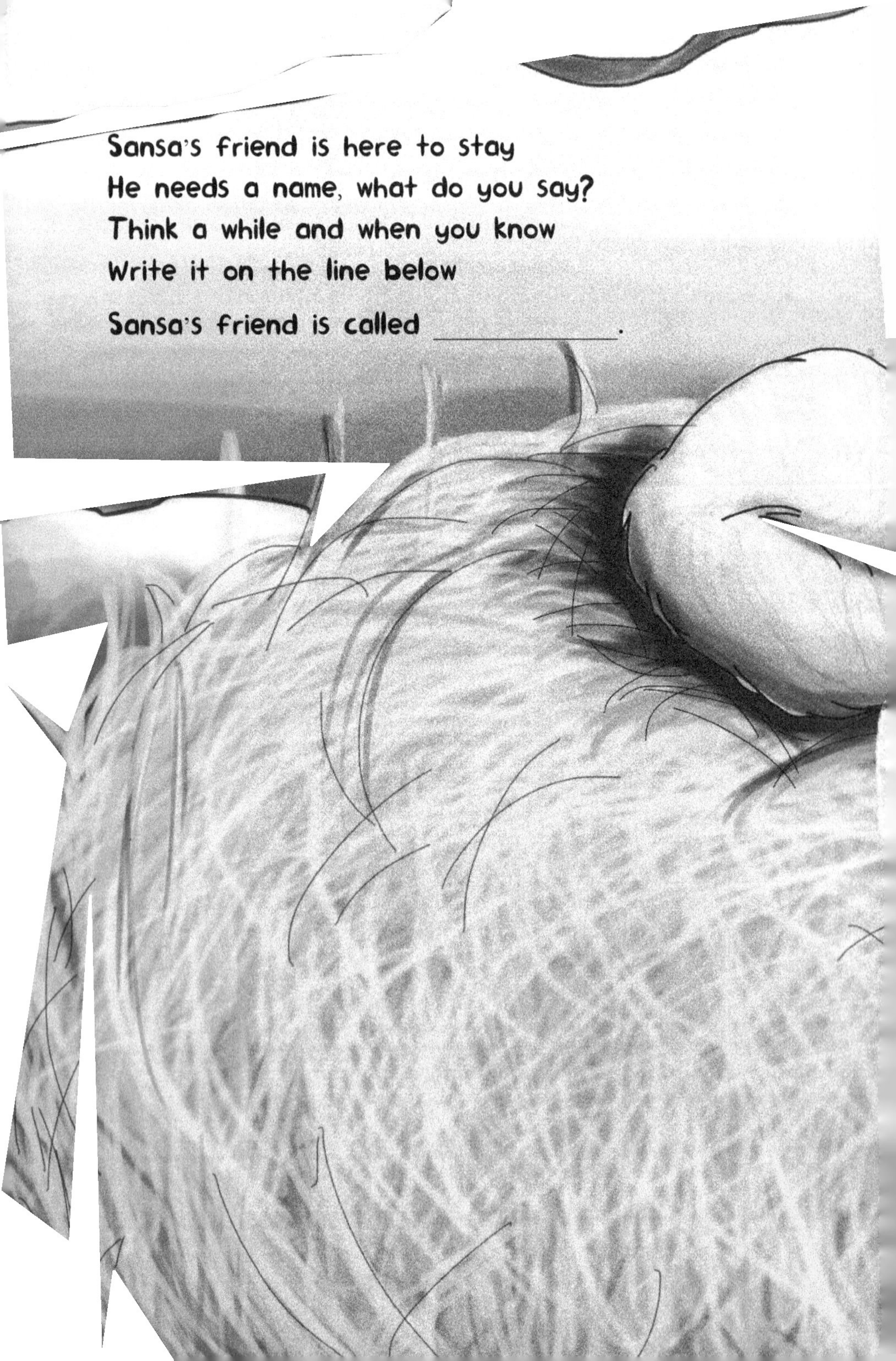

Sansa's friend is here to stay
He needs a name, what do you say?
Think a while and when you know
Write it on the line below

Sansa's friend is called ______________.

Sansa says that if you find
Someone alone you must be kind
Give a friendly wave and say
'Hello, would you like to play?'

CPSIA information can be obtained
at www.ICGtesting.com
Printed in the USA
BVHW01s2337170918
527713BV00007B/123/P